There's a Mouse in My New House

By Hannah Sheridan

Illustrations by Miles DiCarlo

Independently published by Writers Castle Publishing.

writerscastlepublishing@gmail.com

ISBN: 9781796678963

For Jane

"Help, get out!" I heard a shout,
from my mum downstairs in my new house.

She was in the basement, but her cry was loud!
A screeching, squealing kind of sound.

So,

I rushed

downstairs...

Careful not

to stumble.

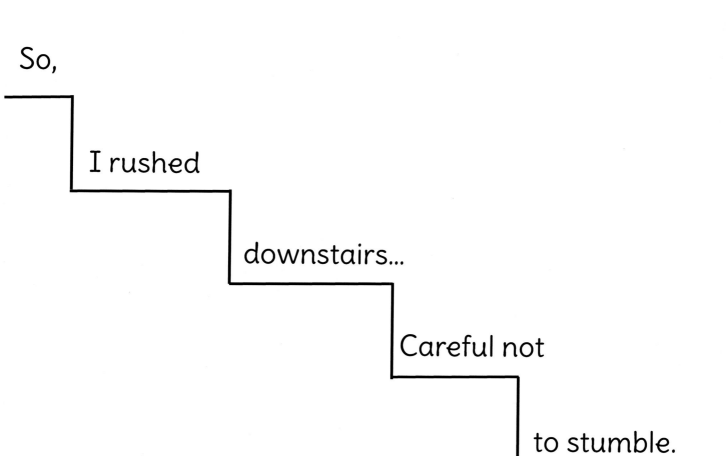

Past the furnace

that was beginning to rumble.

Over a GIGANTIC pile of wood,

to the basement door, where my mum stood.

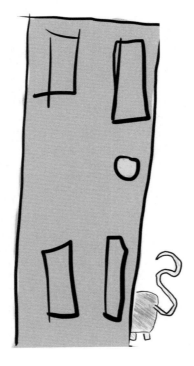

There in the dark twitched a tiny tail.
Was this the cause of mum's screeching wail?

It was a mouse! That's right, it really was true.
A mouse in my house, a house that is new!

Squeak!

It looked pretty scared, and my mum did too.
"GET IT OUT QUICK!" She bellowed
"While I hide in the loo."

My mum disappeared, leaving the case in my hands.

"SHOOOOOOOOOOOOO, and get out!" I tried to demand.

But the mouse didn't budge... Not even an inch!

In fact, it got closer and gave me a pinch!

"Ouch!" I shouted, jumping back in fright.

"I'm sorry," squeaked the mouse, "but you are just not right."

Shocked as I was that this mouse had a voice, I asked what he meant (I had no choice)!

"What do you mean, little mouse?" I replied, frustrated.

"Why it's YOU who must leave.
It's MY house you've invaded"

"Your house? I'm terribly sorry, but you must be mistaken. This house was built for me, and the space is all taken."

"It wasn't always here, though." The mouse advised.
"Why look behind here and you will be surprised."

I took a deep breath
and glanced down at
the ground.
Through the door by
the washer and that's
when I found...

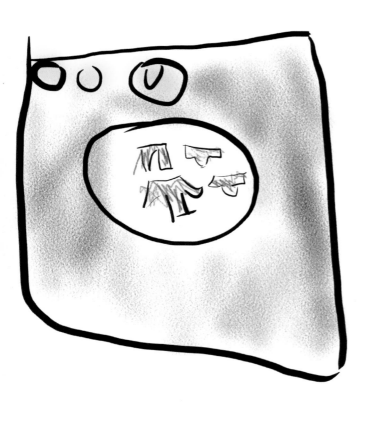
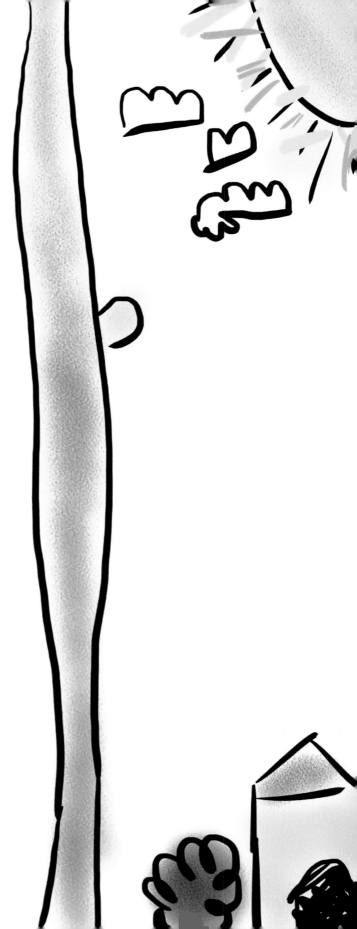

The smallest house I ever did see...

Hiding a little mouse family of three.

"There!" he cried, and he stomped
as he said it.
"We've lived here for years, now
please don't forget it."

"I'm sorry, mouse you are right it's not fair, keep out of sight and I guess we can share."

The tiny mouse smirked and turned on its way, and I haven't seen it again to this day.

The years have flown by and it stays out of sight, only appearing in the dead of night...

40937385R00015